P9-DDR-210

Aphids are very small insects.
They suck the juice from leaves,
and then the leaves die.
Ladybugs eat aphids.
That's good for trees, shrubs, and
other plants that have leaves.
To the ladybugs I have dedicated this book.
Three cheers for them!

Copyright secured 1977
in countries signatory to
International Copyright Union.
All rights reserved.
Printed in Hong Kong.

CIP information in back of book.

The Grouchy Ladybug

Eric Carle

HarperCollins*Publishers*

It was night, and some fireflies danced around the moon.

At five o'clock in the morning the sun came up.
A friendly ladybug flew in from the left. It saw a leaf with many aphids on it,
and decided to have them for breakfast.
But just then a grouchy ladybug flew in from the right.
It too saw the aphids and wanted them for breakfast.

"Good morning," said the friendly ladybug.
"Go away!" shouted the grouchy ladybug. "I want those aphids."
"We can share them," suggested the friendly ladybug.
"No. They're mine, all mine," screamed the grouchy ladybug.
"Or do you want to fight me for them?"

"If you insist," answered the friendly ladybug sweetly.
It looked the other bug straight in the eye.
The grouchy ladybug stepped back.
It looked less sure of itself.
"Oh, you're not big enough for me to fight," it said.
"Then why don't you pick on somebody bigger?"
"I'll do that!" screeched the grouchy ladybug.
"I'll show you!" It puffed itself up and flew off.

At six o'clock
it met a yellow jacket.
"Hey you," said the
grouchy ladybug.
"Want to fight?"
"If you insist,"
said the yellow jacket,
showing its stinger.
"Oh, you're not big
enough," said the grouchy
ladybug and flew off.

At two o'clock
it met a gorilla.
"Hey you," said the
grouchy ladybug.
"Want to fight?"
"If you insist," said
the gorilla, beating
its chest.
"Oh, you're not big
enough," said the
grouchy ladybug
and flew off.

At three o'clock
it ran into a
rhinoceros.
"Hey you," said the
grouchy ladybug.
"Want to fight?"
"If you insist," said
the rhinoceros,
lowering its horn.
"Oh, you're not big
enough," said the
grouchy ladybug
and flew off.

At four o'clock
it encountered
an elephant.
"Hey you," said the
grouchy ladybug. "Want
to fight?"
"If you insist," said the
elephant, raising its
trunk and showing its
big tusks.
"Oh, you're not big enough,"
said the grouchy ladybug
and flew off.

At five o'clock
it met a whale.
"Hey you," said the
grouchy ladybug.
"Want to fight?"
But the whale
didn't answer at all.
"You're not big
enough anyway," said
the grouchy ladybug
and flew off.

At five fifteen the grouchy ladybug said to
one of the whale's flippers, "Hey you, want to fight?"

But it got no answer. So it flew on.

At five thirty the grouchy ladybug said to the whale's fin, "Hey you, want to fight?"

But it got no answer. So it flew on.

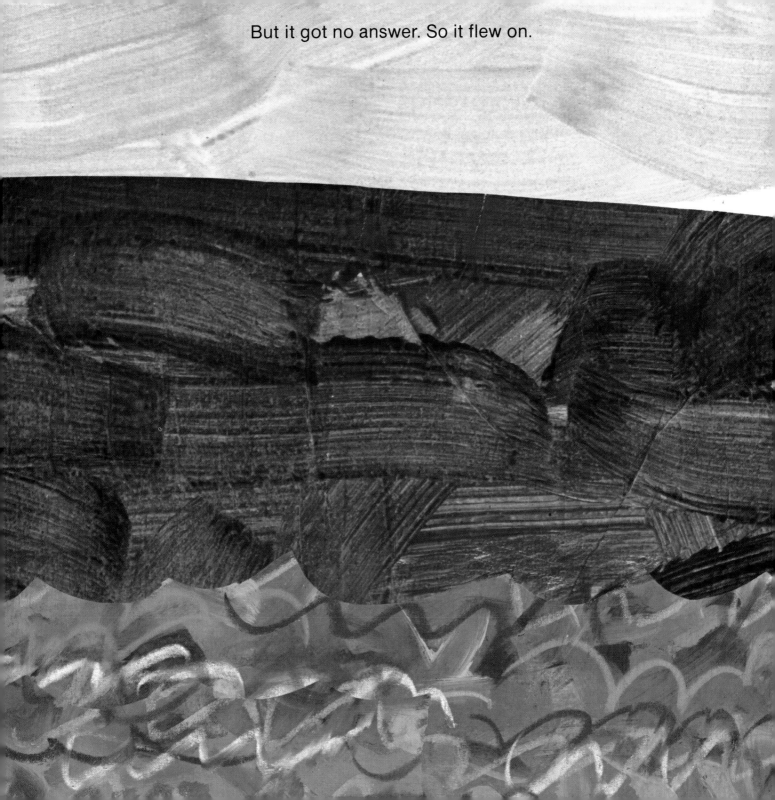

At a quarter to six the grouchy ladybug said to the whale's tail, "Hey you, want to fight?"

...that it flew across the sea and across the land.

At six o'clock the grouchy ladybug arrived right back where it had started from.

"Ah, here you are again," said the friendly ladybug. "You must be hungry. There are still some aphids left. You can have them for dinner."
"Oh, thank you," said the wet, tired, and hungry ladybug.

Soon all the aphids were gone.
"Thank you," said the leaf.
"You are welcome," answered both ladybugs, and they went to sleep.
The fireflies, who had been sleeping all day, came out to dance around the moon.